THE ADVENTURES OF FIREMAN

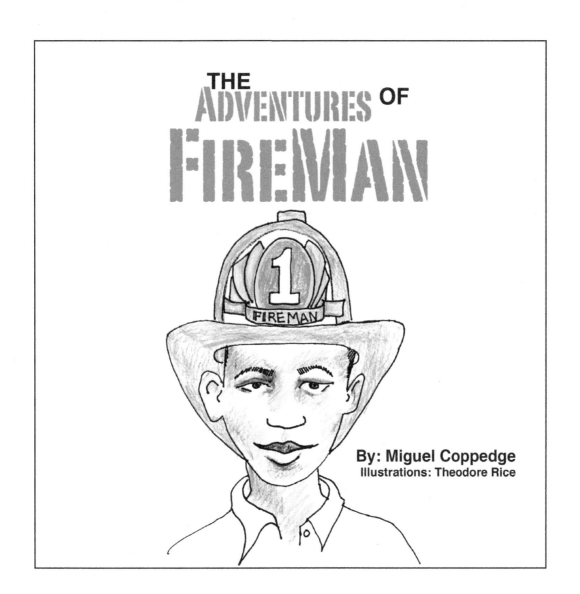

By: Miguel Coppedge

Illustrations: Theodore Rice

Halo
Publishing International

ISBN: 978-1-61244-372-0

Printed in the United States of America

Published by Halo Publishing International
1100 NW Loop 410
Suite 700 - 176
San Antonio, Texas 78213
Toll Free 1-877-705-9647
Website: www.halopublishing.com
E-mail: contact@halopublishing.com

I dedicate this book to my mommy Yolanda Coppedge, my daddy Magale Narce, my granddaddy Van Coppedge, my 3rd grade teacher Mrs. Robinson, Mrs. Crystal and Mr. Kerron from the George Ferris Boys & Girls Clubhouse #6, Mr. Theodore Rice for the Awesome illustrations, and last but not least, President Barack Obama! Thank you all for believing in me. I love you!

Miguel

One day a guy named Kris Schmoove came to earth in 1998. He was from where Superman is from, Planet Krypton.

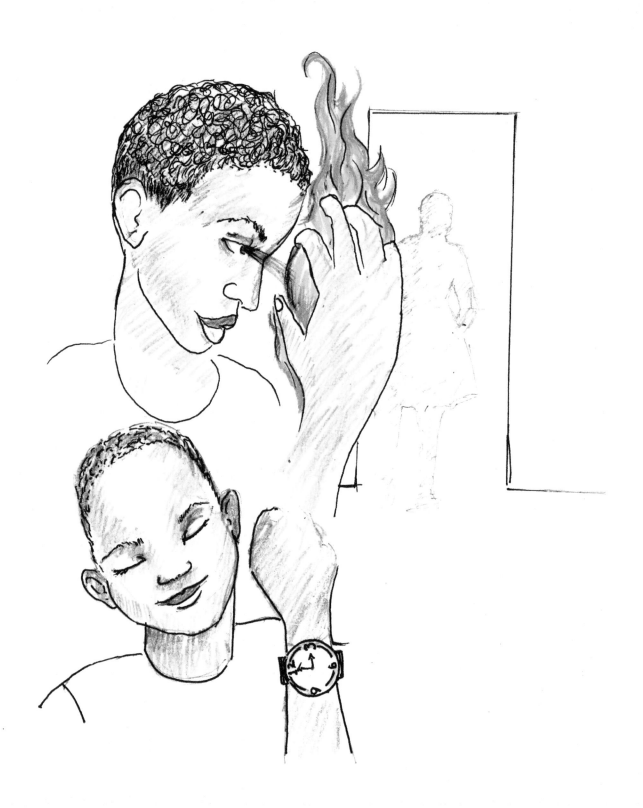

Kris Schmoove discovered that he had super fire powers when he was nine years old. He kept it a secret until he was 10 years old. He finally told his parents and his best friend Rico G. Rico told Kris that he has super powers also. He has the power to slow down time.

Rico became Kris' sidekick and together they fought crime. At 10 years old, Kris and Rico became the youngest super heroes in the world.

FireMan and The Time Slower loved being super heroes. They helped protect people from evil and they received all kinds of awards and good stuff.

Their arch enemy was called The Destroyer. He was a really, really, really bad guy and destroyed anything he didn't like.

One of The Destroyer's thugs called "Bang" almost killed Rico The Time Slower. He was called "Bang" because he liked to bang things up.

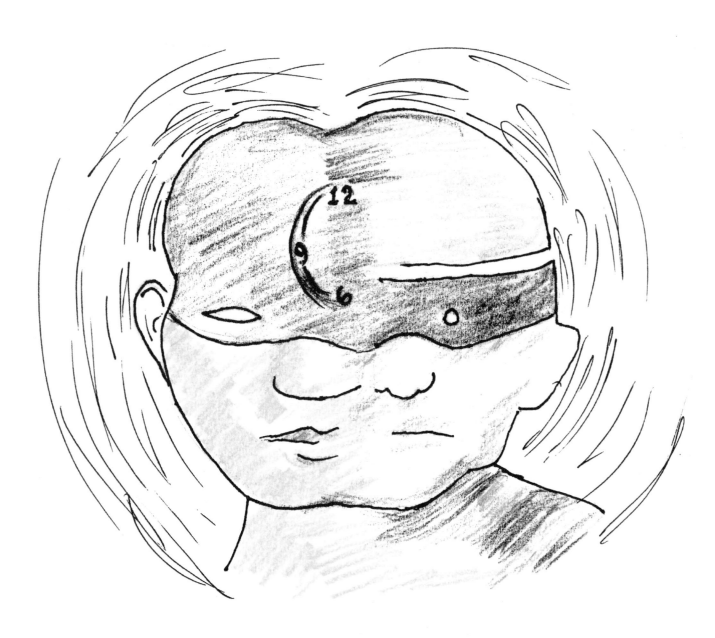

Bang had the power to interchange bodies. When Bang caught The Time Slower, he interchanged his body into his. The Time Slower's body went nuts!

So that meant a job for FIREMAN! Up, up and away! Here comes FireMan to save the day!

FireMan and Bang fought and fought until the next day. Bang was defeated by FireMan and The Time Slower got his body back.

FireMan and The Time Slower set off to find The Destroyer. They didn't want him to destroy anything else in the world. "He must be stopped!" FireMan said.

The Destroyer knew they were coming. He hit The Time Slower with a bat. That didn't hurt him at all. He used his power and slowed down time and FireMan used his fire power to defeat The Destroyer.

The world was safe again. Kris Schmoove "FireMan" and Rico G. "The Time Slower" decided to retire from being super heroes and focused on just being teenagers.

"It is not over FireMan! We will meet again! Ha! Ha! Ha!" said The Destroyer.

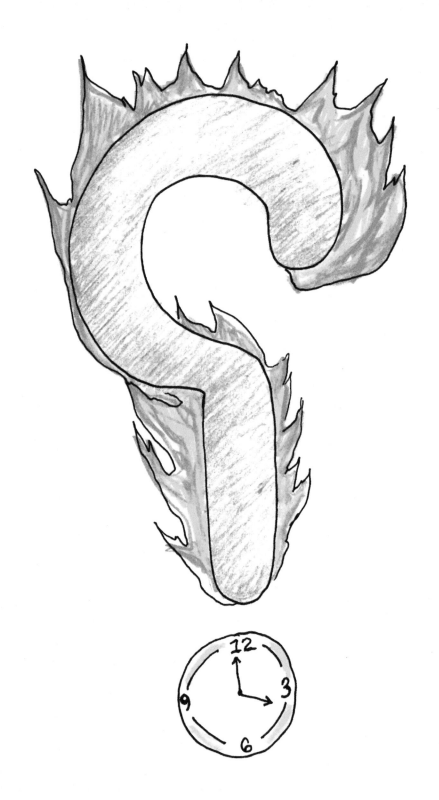

Will Kris Schmoove and Rico G. come out of retirement? Stay tuned!

CPSIA information can be obtained
at www.ICGtesting.com
Printed in the USA
BVOW05*1655141116
467621BV00002B/1/P